D1402028

TEEN LIFE™

FREQUENTLY ASKED QUESTIONS ABOUT

Dating

Vanessa
Baish

ROSEN
PUBLISHING®

New York

Published in 2007 by The Rosen Publishing Group, Inc.
29 East 21st Street, New York, NY 10010

First Edition

Library of Congress Cataloging-in-Publication Data

Baish, Vanessa.
Frequently asked questions about dating / Vanessa Baish. — 1st ed.
p. cm.—(FAQ: teen life).
Includes bibliographical references and index.
ISBN-13: 978-1-4042-1969-4 (alk. paper)
ISBN-10: 1-4042-1969-2 (alk. paper)
1. Dating (Social customs)—Juvenile literature. 2. Interpersonal
relations in adolescence—Juvenile literature. I. Title.
HQ801.B126 2007
306.730835—dc22

2006033584

Manufactured in the United States of America

Contents

Introduction

Dating can be an exciting and fun experience. It gives you a chance to meet new people and try new things. While you are getting to know someone, you also get to know yourself. You can decide what is important to you and what is not so important and learn about the kind of people you like and respect and those you don't. Dating is a big part of growing up.

Dating can also be confusing. There are a lot of choices and decisions to make, and you may not be sure how to proceed. Maybe you have a crush on someone and don't know how to tell that person. Or maybe someone has a crush on you and you aren't sure what to do. You may be afraid to ask someone on a date or to go on a date if someone asks you. What will you talk about? Where will you go? Will you have to or want to kiss? Will you want to have sex?

Dating is like riding a roller coaster. You want to try it, and you think you'll like it, but you aren't sure exactly what to expect. While it's happening, your stomach feels funny, your palms are sweaty, and you're scared. Then you suddenly realize that you are laughing, having fun, and enjoying yourself.

Spending time with someone who you think of as more than a friend can often lead to a romantic relationship. This experience is an exciting part of growing up. In such a relationship, you have to learn how to balance the time spent with your boyfriend or girlfriend with everything else in your

Friendship is the basis of a good dating relationship. So, it's natural for romantic feelings to arise between friends.

life, such as school, friends, and family. You have to figure out when the right time is for you to get serious. You can talk about things such as dating exclusively (which means you go out only with each other and do not date other people), whether or not to become sexual, and your future together. You might also have to figure out when a relationship isn't working and if it is time to say good-bye.

While you are dating, just like riding a roller coaster, you also have to think about safety. You need to look out for yourself. That means learning about things such as date rape, birth control, sexually transmitted diseases (STDs), and physical and mental abuse. These things happen in all kinds of relationships, even between teenagers. You need to know how to be smart, stay safe, and get help if you need it.

Maybe you don't even want to date yet. Maybe your parents won't allow it. That's okay, too. Every person is different, and different people start dating at different times. Some people do a lot of dating before they find someone with whom they want to have a relationship. Sometimes those relationships work, and other times they don't. Others find one person, date him or her, start a relationship, and live happily ever after.

When you are in a relationship, you learn about your values and your emotions. Honesty, trust, and respect are important aspects of any close friendship or relationship. And though dating and romantic relationships aren't always predictable or easy, they are enriching and an important part of growing up.

WHEN SHOULD I DATE?

You may be asking yourself, "What does 'dating' mean, anyway?" The truth of the matter is that dating means many different things, depending on whom you talk to. How do you know if you are dating someone? Well, there isn't an easy answer to this question.

You can date someone you see every day or just once a week. You can also date someone who lives next door, across the country, or even across the world. You can date more than one person or commit yourself to just one guy or girl. You may go out on dates to places like the movies or the local diner. If you don't drive or don't have access to a car, you may just hang out together at school and at friends' houses. And just because you are doing these things with someone doesn't always mean that you are dating. Maybe the two of you are just good friends.

When it comes to dating, it's important for friends to tell each other how they feel about their relationship.

Confused? If you are, that's okay. Dating is complicated. The most important thing to remember is to talk to your partner. Make sure that you both agree on the kind of relationship you have. It is easy to hurt someone's feelings if you are not communicating clearly.

If you're not sure where you stand with someone, don't be afraid to ask him or her. Find out what kind of relationship the person thinks you two have and what kind of relationship he or she wants to have with you in the future. Whether you decide to date or to be just friends, it is important to have an honest, open relationship and good communication.

How Do I Know If I'm Ready?

As a teenager, you are probably pretty curious about sex. Your body is changing, and you may be experiencing some emotions that are new to you. Suddenly, you may find yourself sexually attracted to others.

Along with these physical changes come many emotional changes. You may feel the need to try new things and be more independent. You may want to meet new people and start new relationships. Dating helps to teach you how to treat other people and also allows you to discover how you want to be treated by others. Through dating, you can grow as a person and become more confident, self-sufficient, and independent.

Some people begin dating in their early teens, whereas others wait until their twenties. Peer pressure—when people around you pressure you to do things that you wouldn't normally do—can be tough to deal with. Though it can be hard to stand up for what you believe in, and for what you want to do and not do, ultimately, others will respect you for making your own choices. Don't let others make decisions for you. If you don't want to date now, do not let other people's opinions sway you. And if you do want to date, remember that in order for it to be a positive experience, you have to be mature enough to know what you want.

In any relationship, especially a romantic one, it is important to be sensitive. This means being able to respect someone else's thoughts, feelings, and opinions, regardless of whether or not you agree with him or her. You also should be able to communicate effectively with the person you date. You should be honest with each other and try to resolve your differences. Everyone feels hurt, jealous, and angry sometimes. Solving problems together makes a relationship stronger.

When you build a new relationship, you are also building trust. And with this bond should come comfort. If you are shy and nervous and find dating uncomfortable, maybe you should wait until you feel ready.

Does all of this sound hard to do? It is, but you don't need to do it all at once. People spend entire lifetimes learning to respect, trust, and communicate with the ones they care about. If you are willing to jump in and get started with all this, you are probably ready to date.

Parents? Not a Problem

Your parents may want to be involved in your social life. If this is the case and you have decided that you are ready to date, talk

You are very important to your parents. Don't be surprised if they want to be involved in your decisions regarding dating.

to your parents about your decision. It is better to be up front, rather than sneaking around without their knowledge.

Explain why you feel ready to start dating. Presenting a thoughtful argument for dating will show them that you take it seriously and that you intend to behave responsibly. Your parents may put some restrictions on you, such as a curfew or deciding how often you can date, where you are allowed to go, and if you can use the car. By showing your parents that you acknowledge their concerns, you will earn their trust.

Sometimes parents decide that teens should not date. Depending on your age, religion, and background, your parents may have certain ideas about when dating is appropriate. If your parents forbid you to date, ask them why. Perhaps you can address their concerns. If not, it is best to obey them. Disobeying your parents will cause them to lose trust in you and to doubt your maturity. If they do not want you to date, wait a few months and then discuss dating with them again. Your responsible behavior may convince them that you are ready to date after all.

WHAT IS
A CRUSH?

It always happens when you least expect it. There you are, minding your own business, and you look up and see Him. Or maybe you're hanging out with your friends and suddenly She walks by. Time stops, and the world around you fades away. That's it—you have a crush.

Crushes

When you have a crush, meaning that you like someone from afar, you usually want to get to know the object of your affection better. However, you may not be sure how to go about this. Everyone gets crushes. Sometimes teens have crushes on people who are much **older than they are, such as a teacher, coach, or friend's mom or dad.**

Crushes are fun, but they can be scary, too. The uncertainty about what to do about your crush can be exciting.

Crushes are very intense, but most last only a short while. That "perfect" person won't stay perfect forever!

As long as you do not become obsessed, crushes are a safe way to get used to all the feelings that attraction brings. You may be tongue-tied and terrified around your crush. That's okay; more than likely he or she will not know this is going on. That is why crushes are fun. But remember, crushes are not the same as relationships; you may admire someone without the feeling being returned. If you do start to date, you will experience some of the same feelings you had during your crush. This is good because you will be able to recognize the feelings that you are having and they will not seem so strange.

Same-Sex Crushes

Many people have crushes on someone of the same sex. Girls can get crushes on other girls and guys can get crushes on other guys. Teens often wonder if having a same-sex crush means that they are gay. Almost everyone has a same-sex crush during his or her life and it is perfectly normal. We get crushes on people we like, admire, and respect, and we want them to like, admire, and respect us. Often same-sex crushes don't have an element of sexual or romantic attraction.

If you do feel sexually or romantically attracted to someone of the same sex, you might be gay. There's nothing wrong with being gay; it's just another way of loving and caring for others.

However, some people think that being gay is wrong or immoral, which can make things hard for gay teens. If you think you are gay, talk about it with someone you trust. He or she can encourage you and help you to find out more about services that support gay people.

Flirting: Do or Don't?

When you have a crush on someone, you want that person to notice you. You want him or her to see that you are smart, funny, attractive, likable, and a good person. Basically, you want your crush to like you as much as you like him or her.

One way to get your crush to notice you—and hopefully like you—is to flirt. Flirting is acting in a way that draws attention to you and is often a playful way of getting to know someone. Both girls and boys flirt.

Flirting does not have to be a big deal. Just saying hello or flashing a smile can get you noticed.

Flirting often gets a bad rap, but it's not necessarily a negative thing. Flirting is a way of subtly expressing your attraction for someone. It's a great way to make a good impression on your crush while you are letting the person know you like him or her.

Sometimes all it takes is letting someone know that you are interested in him or her. Once you get someone's attention, try to get a simple conversation started. If you are relaxed, the two of you will probably enjoy talking to each other. That is the first step. Some people are shy, especially in new situations. But if someone wants to get to know you, too, your attention will please them.

The most important thing to remember while flirting is to be yourself. It is okay to show off all the good qualities you have, but don't go overboard. Good flirting is showing yourself to your best advantage and flattering the other person. Bad flirting is pretending to be someone you're not or making the other person uncomfortable. If you act less intelligent, capable, sensitive, or thoughtful than you really are, you're not showing your crush the real you. When it comes to flirting, it can be hard to know where to draw the line. Just be yourself. You are smart, talented, attractive, and fun—there's no need to act differently.

Okay, so you've decided that you are ready to date, and your parents approve. You have found the guy or girl that you would like to get to know better. You have made the first step in getting to know your crush. Maybe you have tried flirting, maybe not. Are you ready for the next big step—the date itself?

chapter
three

HOW DO YOU MAKE A DATE?

Just like writing a paper, the hardest part of dating is getting started. Many teens say they don't date because they are afraid to ask someone out. Years ago, it was mainly guys who asked girls for a date. Today, however, girls are taking charge and asking guys out, too.

If you want to ask someone out, it may be easier if you plan in advance what you are going to say. Have an idea of where you would like to go on the date. Ask your date to do something specific, like go to a movie, a school dance, or a party. You will also want to speak to the person alone. Asking for a date is hard enough without a group of snickering guys or giggling girls peering over your shoulder.

Let's be real—it is hard to ask someone out on a date! You are making yourself vulnerable and risking rejection. After all, the person could say no. But he or she could say

A first date should be fun and relaxed. You'll have a much better time if you do a simple activity you both enjoy.

yes, too! The best advice: Get up your courage, take a deep breath, and ask.

When the Risk Pays Off

You've taken a chance and asked. And the person said yes! Or maybe someone has asked you for a date and you've said yes. Now what? Whether you have been asked out or you've done the asking, you'll want to be part of planning the date.

First dates don't have to be elaborate, expensive events. You can do something as simple and inexpensive as going to a

Myths and Facts

About Dating

 Rapists are people who hide in the bushes or the shadows of parking garages, waiting to leap out at you. Fact ➥ Almost two-thirds of all rapes are committed by someone known to the victim— 67 percent of sexual assaults are perpetrated by non-strangers: 47 percent of perpetrators are friends or acquaintances of the victim; 17 percent are intimates; and 3 percent are relatives.

 **Everyone is having sex but me.** Fact ➥ Although it may seem like everyone is having sex, fewer than half of high school students have had sex.

All birth control is the same. I'm safe as long as I'm using something. Fact ➥ While spermicides seem like a good alternative to condoms for preventing pregnancy, they can actually irritate the skin, making it easier to transmit disease. Condoms are still the best method of birth control and disease prevention.

All first dates should be going to a movie or out to dinner. Fact ➾ A date can be whatever activity you and your date like to do. You could have a picnic, go for a hike, go to a sporting event, or visit an art gallery. Just be sure you will both have fun.

 If you don't want to date, you're weird. Fact ➾ Completely not true! Some people would rather spend time with their friends or alone than spend time with a romantic partner. Just like any other activity, some people like to date and some people don't.

friend's party or meeting at a school football game. The important thing is that you both agree on what to do.

If you have asked someone to go to a movie, find out what kind of films the person likes and then decide on a film together. If someone has asked you to dinner, don't be shy about sharing your likes and dislikes. If you are a vegetarian, do not agree to go to a steakhouse. If you hate seafood and your date suggests going to a restaurant that specializes in fish dishes, speak up. Do not be afraid of hurting the other person's feelings. After all, if you don't enjoy the movie or the meal, you won't have a good time.

Consider planning your first date with a group of people. It makes conversation a lot easier, and the date may go more

One-on-one dates are fine, but the conversation often flows better when you arrange a date with other friends.

smoothly with others around. Dating in a group takes the pressure off you and your date. You can go on a double date with another couple or just hang out with a bunch of friends. Rent a video together, hang out in the park, or pick another group activity. It's easier to be yourself when you are around people you are familiar with.

After picking the event together, decide on a time. Do you want to see a movie at night or an afternoon matinee? On a school night or a weekend? You will also need to think about transportation. Who is going to drive? If neither of you is old enough to drive, you'll have to arrange a way to get there and back or make a plan to meet. When planning your date, keep your parents' rules in mind. After all, you don't want to break curfew or borrow the car without asking and end up grounded.

Dealing with Rejection

Unfortunately, your crush may say no to a date. Dating disappointments happen to everyone, but they hurt just the same. If someone turns you down for a date, it is best to simply say okay and walk away. People have all sorts of reasons for not going on a date, and often those reasons have nothing to do with you. Maybe that person isn't allowed to date or maybe he or she already has a boyfriend or girlfriend. Sometimes a person simply isn't interested in you romantically.

If you question the girl in your chemistry class about why she turned you down for a date, you are likely to end up with hurt feelings. If she is trying to be considerate, don't make her explain in detail why she can't or doesn't want to go out with you. Also, don't argue. You won't change her mind, and you will both end up feeling very uncomfortable.

What if someone asks you out on a date and you don't want to go? It's perfectly acceptable to say no, and it's the best thing to do. Dating someone because you don't want to say no or because you feel bad for that person isn't fair to either of you. By accepting the date, you would be giving that person the impression that you are romantically interested when you aren't. Instead, be polite and say, "No, thanks."

A kiss can be an appropriate way to show your affection if both of you are having a great time on a date.

Don't make excuses for saying no, unless they're true. If you tell Mike that you can't go out with him on Saturday night because you already planned to go to a movie with your best friend, he might assume that you would go if you were not busy and will probably ask you out again. What will you say then? A firm, polite "No, thank you" will let him down gently without giving him false hope.

The Big Moment

A word about kissing: Despite what some people say, there is no rule about kissing on the first date. Do what feels right for you. If you like the person and want to kiss him or her, make sure it's okay with the other person and then go ahead. If you don't feel ready yet, you don't have to kiss anyone. And don't be insulted if your date doesn't try to kiss you. If the time is right, the kiss will happen.

WHAT IS BEING IN A RELATIONSHIP ALL ABOUT?

We all have many different kinds of relationships. You have relationships with parents, brothers and/or sisters, and other relatives. You also have relationships with friends, acquaintances, peers, coworkers, team members, and teachers. Here, when we talk about a relationship, it refers to a romantic relationship between two people who care for each other.

After two people have gone on a few dates, they usually realize that they are getting to know one another better. At this stage, a relationship is starting to develop. In a relationship, you can learn more about your partner's likes and dislikes, family and friends, hopes, dreams, fears, and sense of humor.

However, in any relationship in which you share your innermost thoughts and feelings, you are also vulnerable, meaning that you are at risk of getting hurt. You are sharing

Ten Great Questions to Ask When You're Thinking About Dating

1 How old is old enough to date?

2 My parents don't think I am old enough to date, but I do think I am old enough. Can I convince them that they can trust my judgment? How?

3 I want to ask someone in one of my classes out, but I am afraid they will say no. What do I say? What do I do if they say no?

4 I have been dating the same person for a few weeks/months/years and we are thinking about having sex. How do we know when we are ready? What if one of us is but the other isn't?

5 I don't want to have sex with the person I am dating and s/he is pressuring me. How do I get him/her to stop? What if s/he won't?

6 We decided we are ready to have sex and we want to be safe. Where can we go for information about safe sex practices?

7 My boy/girlfriend and I have been together for a while but I don't think I want to date him/her any longer. How do I know when the relationship is over? How do I break up with him/her?

8 I recently broke up with my boy/girlfriend and now I have to see him/her all the time in school and it's hard. What can I do to not feel bad when I see this person?

9 I don't think my friend is being very smart about his/her relationships. Should I say something? What can I say without making him/her angry?

10 All my friends are dating and I'm not. Is something wrong with me?

private parts of yourself with someone. A relationship can be scary, but it can also be wonderful. Being part of a healthy relationship can teach you a lot about yourself.

The Right Stuff

Boyfriends and girlfriends have all sorts of ways of relating to and behaving with each other. You may know some couples who are very serious and others who joke around a lot. Maybe you know some couples who spend lots of time together, whereas other couples see each other only once in a while. Different people have different ways of being together, but a few elements are key to all healthy relationships.

You know someone is special when you talk to him or her about things that you don't discuss with any of your other friends.

Communication

In a healthy relationship, couples talk openly to one another. They share their thoughts, opinions, emotions, and ideas. Couples even tell each other when they feel hurt, angry, ashamed, or jealous. It is not always easy to share your feelings with someone else, but it is very important. By revealing more about yourselves, you get to know each other better. By sharing your problems, hurts, and frustrations, you can then figure out a way to resolve them together. That makes your relationship stronger.

By dating someone, you discover new things about him or her. Your relationship will teach you new things about yourself, too.

Individuality

It is important to be comfortable with who you are, especially when you are in a relationship. Each person brings something unique and special to the relationship. Couples complement one another by playing off each other's strengths and weaknesses. Think about the qualities or character traits that you like best about your girlfriend or boyfriend.

Honesty and Trust

Honesty builds trust, and trust is an essential part of a happy relationship. Couples need to be truthful with each other and up front about problems and other complicated issues. As a couple, you rely on each other. It is important that you and your partner trust each other and believe that the other will be there for emotional support in times of need.

Respect

To show respect means that you value the opinions, beliefs, and ideas of someone else. Basically, you believe in that person. People in healthy relationships respect one another. They do not purposely hurt, put down, or upset each other. Though they may not always see eye-to-eye about everything, they respect their partner's opinion.

Keeping It in Perspective

It's easy to get wrapped up in a relationship when you think that you have found the perfect girl or guy. You are getting to know each other better and

having a great time. It sometimes seems as if nothing is as much fun as being with your boyfriend or girlfriend. However, it is important to keep things in perspective. You need to find a balance between your relationship and all the other aspects of your life. These include your family, friends, school, a part-time job, pets, hobbies, and other interests.

Before you get too caught up in a new relationship, take a moment to think about what makes you unique. What are your talents and your strengths? Are you a musician, a writer, an athlete,

Dating should not cause you to abandon activities you enjoy. It's healthy to view your relationship as one important part of a busy, well-rounded life.

or just an all-around fun, interesting person? Do not neglect the rest of your life. You will need to learn how to balance your responsibilities.

Your talents and hobbies make you happy, so do not stop pursuing them. Also, you should be careful not to neglect the people who care about you. With your family and good friends by your side, providing comfort and support, you can probably make it through anything.

You don't need to spend all of your time with your boyfriend or girlfriend in order for your relationship to be strong. The more you do and learn individually, the more you will have to contribute to your relationship. People who truly care about you want you to be the best, most talented, and most interesting person you can be.

chapter
five

HOW CAN I BE SAFE AND SMART ABOUT DATING?

Dating and relationships are an important part of growing up—something that many teens want to experience. However, there are some concerns that you should be aware of in regard to dating and relationship safety. If you want to make the most of your teen years, you need to be smart and stay safe.

Date and Acquaintance Rape

Date rape occurs when two people are on a date and one person forces the other to have sex. Acquaintance rape means that the rapist is someone the victim knows but is not necessarily dating. Both guys and girls can be date rapists and both guys and girls can be victims. However, in most date rape situations, females are the victims and males are the aggressors.

Some date rapists are violent criminals who threaten to hurt or kill their victims. More often, date rapists are males who force women to have sex by pressuring and physically intimidating them. For both people involved in a relationship, regardless of whether they are male or female, it is extremely important to be sensitive to what your partner wants. If your date or partner says that he or she does not want to have sex, respect that choice. Don't put sexual pressure on your partner. Instead, talk about what you both want and try to figure out a way to meet each other's needs.

It is especially important for women to be very clear about their sexual choices. If you don't want to have sex, tell your date "no" firmly. If he persists, leave or call for help. Also, you are allowed to change your mind, even at the last minute. Maybe you thought you wanted to have sex, but then you realized you didn't. Sex is not something you should engage in because you feel guilty. You can always say no—no matter what. And remember, whatever the circumstances, rape is never your fault.

Dating Smarts

To stay safe, you'll need to be cautious on dates, especially when you don't know the person well. By following the tips below, you can avoid many dangerous situations.

- Avoid being alone with someone you don't know well or trust completely.
- Drive yourself to and from a date or arrange transportation beforehand. Don't get into a car alone with someone you don't know well.

Driving her own car allows a young woman to play it safe when dating a guy she doesn't know well.

- Always bring money on a date in case you need to call someone to pick you up or pay for transportation home.
- Don't drink alcohol or take drugs and don't stay with a date who does. People under the influence of alcohol and drugs make poor decisions.
- If your date seems angry, violent, abusive, or unstable, leave immediately.
- Trust your instincts. If you feel uncomfortable or frightened, call for help or get out of the situation immediately.

Abusers often use charm, promises, and pleading to keep the other person in the abusive relationship.

Recognizing an Abusive Relationship

More than 70,000 women are assaulted each year; more than two-thirds of them are under eighteen. Also, approximately one of every three high school students—both male and female—has been involved in an abusive relationship. Teens who plan to date need to know the signs of an **abusive relationship**.

An abusive relationship is one in which one person mistreats the other in some way. The abuse can be physical, sexual, or emotional. Abusers often have other problems in their lives. They may have emotional problems, drug or alcohol problems, or difficulties at home. Even so, there is no excuse for abuse. Hurting someone is definitely not the right way to deal with your own problems and frustrations. Similarly, if someone has abused you in any way, it is not your fault. No one asks to be hurt, and no one deserves it. You need to get away from your abuser and get help.

Help Is Out There

If you have been raped or abused, you need to get help right away. You may feel as though you are all alone, but you aren't. Many people have experienced date or acquaintance rape and have survived. All sorts of resources are available to help you. First of all, you need to get to a safe place away from your attacker or abuser. Tell a parent, friend, teacher, or someone else you trust what has happened. He or she can encourage and support you while you get help.

If you've been raped or physically or sexually abused, call the police and get medical attention. Eventually you'll have to tell your parents. Remember, you have done nothing wrong. There is no reason to feel guilty or ashamed. If you think you will have trouble telling your parents, ask someone to be there with you to help you.

People who have been raped or abused have to cope with feelings such as anger, shame, embarrassment, depression, and sometimes even thoughts of suicide. Talking about what you are feeling is the best way to handle your emotions. You can speak to a guidance counselor, therapist, or someone else you think can help you get through this. Many people have survived rape and abuse; you can, too.

Chapter Six

WHAT HAPPENS WHEN A RELATIONSHIP GETS SERIOUS?

After you have been dating the same person for a while, there may come a time when you discover that your relationship is getting more serious. The two of you are probably spending more time together, you tell each other things you would not tell other people, and you are growing closer emotionally. When this happens, you may decide that you want to date only each other. If you decide to date one person exclusively, this means that you and your partner agree that neither of you will date anyone else. Some people call this "going steady." Some couples even exchange small gifts as a sign of their commitment.

Going steady with someone takes your relationship to a new level. It requires even more trust, honesty, and communication. It also requires sacrifice, because each of you is giving up the opportunity to date other people. Before you agree to date someone exclusively, think about how that will change your social life. If you don't think you are ready or think you may get bored or restless dating only one person, you may want to wait.

On the other hand, if you think you are ready to commit to one person, go ahead and do it. Dating exclusively is an important part of learning about yourself and can show you what you need to be in a relationship. It teaches you a lot about the qualities of a healthy and beneficial relationship. You learn a lot about caring for and loving another person.

What About Sex?

Sex is a normal part of a healthy, committed relationship between two mature people. Sex requires maturity and responsibility. If you are thinking about having sex, you will want to give some thought to how sex will change your relationship. You may feel as though everyone but you is having sex, but that is not true. Actually, in North America, the number of teens waiting to have sex until they are in a committed, adult relationship is rising.

If you decide to have sex, you will also want to think about the possible consequences. Sex can result in a sexually transmitted disease (STD) or pregnancy. You should both see a doctor before having sex to make sure that you are not carrying any STDs. Even if you haven't had sex, you could still be infected

These young women anxiously check the results of a home pregnancy test. An unplanned pregnancy can be a very difficult thing to deal with.

with an STD. Any sexual activity where bodily fluids are exchanged, like oral sex, can transmit herpes, for example. But safe sex practices, like using condoms properly, can minimize the possibility of transmitting an STD. If you have had unprotected sex, you are at high risk for STDs. According to the Centers for Disease Control and Prevention (CDC), every year in the United States about one in four sexually active teens contracts a sexually transmitted disease.

Also, what would you do if you found out that you were going to become a parent? How would you deal with the pregnancy?

10 FACTS ABOUT DATING

1 Each year, nine million new cases of STD occur among young people aged fifteen to twenty-four. Sexually active youth have the highest STD rates of any age group in the country.

2 Like adults, many teenagers lack awareness of STDs. More than half of all sexually active teens have never discussed STDs with their partners or health care providers.

3 Many STDs can be "silent," causing no noticeable symptoms in men or women.

4 Between forty thousand and fifty thousand Americans become infected with HIV every year. Half of them are between the ages of thirteen and twenty-four. That means at least two teenagers and young adults in this country are infected with HIV every half hour of every day.

5 Teen pregnancy has declined 28 percent since the early 1990s.

6 One in six American women has been the victim of an attempted or completed rape, and 10 percent of sexual assault victims are men.

7 The good news: Since 1993, rape/sexual assault has decreased by over 64 percent.

8 A German researcher has found that your kissing partner is twice as likely to turn his or her head to the right rather than to the left for smooching. Onur Güntürkün, a psychology professor at the Ruhr-University of Bochum, Germany, came to this conclusion after spying on 224 kissing couples in airports, railway stations, parks, and beaches in the United States, Germany, and Turkey.

9 You burn twenty-six calories in a one-minute kiss.

10 According to *Sperling's Best Places*, Austin, Texas, is the top-rated city for dating. Other highly rated cities include Colorado Springs, San Diego, Raleigh/Durham, and Seattle. The worst city for dating is Kansas City

You and your partner should discuss the possibility of disease and pregnancy before you have sex.

Do you feel as though you can discuss these things with your partner? Are you uncomfortable or embarrassed? If so, then you may not be ready for sex. If you are embarrassed to talk about the possibility of pregnancy, how will you deal with it if it happens? If you are not mature enough to discuss sex, then you are not mature enough to have it.

Staying Safe

If you and your partner do decide that you are ready to have sex, you will want to take precautions against STDs and pregnancy. The male should always wear a condom. It protects against both STDs and pregnancy.

There are many types of STDs. AIDS is by far the most serious STD; there is no cure for it. Sooner or later, AIDS is always fatal. To date, AIDS has killed over 500,000 people in the United States and over twenty-two million people worldwide. The number continues to grow. Other STDs may not be as deadly as the AIDS virus, but they can also have very serious consequences. Some STDs can be treated, but some cannot be cured. If you get genital herpes, genital warts, or hepatitis B, you will have the disease for life. Every time you have sex, your partner will be risking infection. Gonorrhea and chlamydia can cause sterility (make someone unable to have a baby). A woman with syphilis can pass the disease to her unborn child causing birth defects or death. AIDS can also be passed from mother to baby during pregnancy.

Although highly effective, condoms are not 100 percent safe. To decrease your chances of becoming pregnant, you should also use another method of birth control. Some other methods include birth control pills and diaphragms. Together, you and your partner should decide what **kind of birth control you will** use and you should both be aware of how your chosen method of birth control works. Birth control is the responsibility of both partners in a relationship. It's not simply a "man's problem" or a

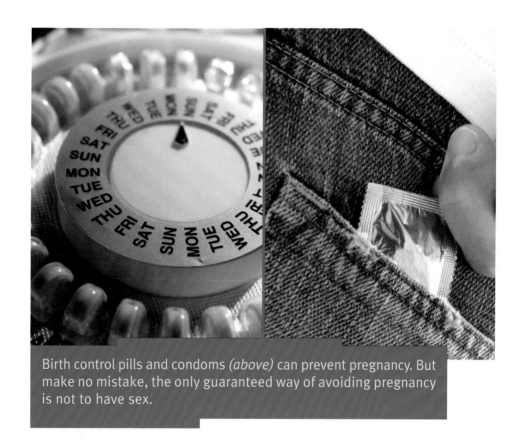

Birth control pills and condoms *(above)* can prevent pregnancy. But make no mistake, the only guaranteed way of avoiding pregnancy is not to have sex.

"woman's problem." If you are old enough to have sex, you're also old enough to do it safely and responsibly.

The Future

As you get older, you will need to think about what role your relationship will play in your future. When you near the end of high school, you will start considering new options—going to college, getting a job, or possibly moving to a new place.

Across the Miles: Long-Distance Relationships

If you or your partner is moving away after high school, you will have to decide if you want to continue your relationship. You can have a long-distance relationship, in which you are still together but don't see each other as often as you would if you lived close. You might only see each other twice a month, once a month, or maybe even only once every few months. Long-distance relationships can be just as happy and healthy as those in which people see each other every day. However, they require an added level of commitment.

Some people decide to stay together even if they are separated by many miles, and their relationships are stronger because of it. Others decide that they can't handle a long-distance relationship. They think they will be lonely or feel left out if they aren't dating someone who lives nearby. Talk to your partner and together decide what is right for you.

A Lifetime Commitment

Some young people are so committed to each other that they decide to get married. Marriage is a huge decision—one that you should consider very carefully. When you get married, you are committing yourself to another person for the rest of your life. You are saying, "This person is the one for me. I don't need to date anymore or try out any more new relationships. I've found my lifetime partner."

Unfortunately, the majority of teenage marriages end in divorce. As you get older, you will grow and change in many

Saying good-bye is hard. When one partner moves far away or leaves for college, young couples have to make some serious decisions.

ways. You are still developing your adult identity in your twenties and even your thirties. Your likes and dislikes, opinions and interests—all these can change radically. The person you thought you wanted to be with forever when you were seventeen might not be the person you want to be with when you are twenty-five.

If you are truly in love with someone, that love will last. Consider waiting a few years before getting married. You don't need to hurry into any big decisions. If you are right for each other, your love won't fade. By waiting to marry, you will give your relationship time to develop and grow. Then, when you're ready to say "I do," it will mean even more.

Chapter seven

HOW DO I DEAL WITH BREAKING UP?

Going on dates and being in a relationship help you to discover what kind of person you feel the most comfortable with. By dating different people, you can see what sort of person fits you best. You will also realize what sort of person you don't want as a partner and discover who isn't right for you. Relationships are learning experiences—even the ones that do not work out the way that you would have liked. All relationships help you figure out what you do and don't want in life.

If you don't have fun with your boyfriend or girlfriend anymore—**if you argue a lot or seem to have grown far apart**—it may be time to reassess your relationship. Analyze the feelings you have for your partner. Does he add something special to your life? Does she make you happy? If you have tried to work things out but you are still not happy, that means that it's time to break up.

Breaking up is never easy. Still, you can take care to avoid saying or doing things that make the split even more hurtful and difficult to accept.

Letting Someone Down Easy

When you are in a relationship with someone, it is because you care about them. Most of the time, even if you want to end a relationship, you probably will still care for your boyfriend or girlfriend and not want to hurt them. It can be difficult to end a relationship in a nonhurtful way. It takes a lot of maturity.

It might be tempting to try to force the relationship to end so that you won't have to actually break up. You may find yourself treating your boyfriend or girlfriend badly or doing things to

Most dating relationships eventually come to an end. Unfortunately, more serious relationships make for more difficult breakups.

push them away. Often you may not realize that you are behaving this way. You may think that if you are inconsiderate enough or mean enough, it will force your boyfriend or girlfriend to break up with you. This plan might work, but you will both feel hurt and angry in the end. Besides, you probably do not really want to mistreat someone you care about. You owe it to your boyfriend or girlfriend to be honest.

When you decide it is time to break up, pick a private place to tell the person. Tell them how you feel and why you think it is best for you to end your relationship. Be honest, but don't hurt

Whether you are the one doing the dumping or the one getting dumped, a breakup is bound to cause anger and confusion.

the person unnecessarily. Be prepared for him or her to ask questions. You also owe it to the person to explain why you are breaking up.

Don't be surprised if he or she gets upset. After you have finished explaining yourself, leave the person alone to deal with the news. It might take a while for it to sink in, and he or she will probably want some space in order to be able to figure things out. However, if the person seems extremely upset and you think that he or she might hurt him- or herself, stay until someone else arrives to help.

Dealing with Getting Dumped

While it is hard to break up with someone, it is even harder to have someone break up with you. People call this "getting dumped" because that is often how it feels. No matter how you think a relationship is going, people rarely expect the breakup when it happens. If someone ends a relationship with you, you need to accept that it is over. The reality of the end of your relationship may take a while to sink in, but you have to respect the other person's decision. Trying to change his mind or win her back will only make things more stressful and uncomfortable for both of you.

If someone breaks up with you, take some time alone to think about the relationship and to figure out how to deal with your feelings. You might see that the decision is the best one for you, too. Or maybe that will take some time. This is a good time to turn to your friends. Everyone, no matter how popular or attractive, has been dumped. Your friends will understand how you feel and will be able to comfort you.

It also helps to keep busy. Remind yourself that you have a very full life, even without the relationship. Remember that you had a great life before you began the relationship. Things can be even better after it's over.

If you truly feel devastated by the breakup, you may want to seek help. Being dumped can make you feel hurt, lonely, and depressed. However, if your feelings are too powerful to handle or last well after the relationship has ended, talk to your parents, a teacher, or a guidance counselor about how you're feeling.

When a relationship ends, you may find yourself with more free time and energy. Staying active will help keep you from dwelling on the breakup.

They can assist you in finding a professional counselor who can help you in handling your feelings.

Moving On

When a relationship ends, it sometimes feels like the end of the world. It takes some time to recover from the hurt and loneliness that comes with a breakup. This is true even when you are the person who ends the relationship.

Remember that being single has lots of advantages. Now is your chance to enjoy them. You can spend time with friends you lost touch with and reconnect with your family. You can get that perfect 4.0 GPA you have been after or try something you've never done before. Take a kickboxing class. Read a really good novel. Start writing in a journal so that you can record your feelings and look back at this time later on. When you are not dating anyone, you will find that you have a lot more free time. Do something fun with it.

abstinence To abstain from sex.

abusive relationship Relationship in which one or both people abuse the other physically, sexually, or emotionally.

acquaintance rape When someone you know forces you to have sex against your will.

birth control Any method used to avoid pregnancy. Examples include condoms, diaphragms, pills, contraceptive creams and jellies, and sponges.

breakup The end of a relationship.

crush Strong romantic attraction to someone who is not aware of your feelings.

date Social engagement between two people who are usually interested in each other romantically.

date rape When a date forces you to have sex against your will.

depressed To feel extremely sad; to be uninterested in your life and your environment; to feel hopeless and/or helpless.

exclusive Only one.

flirt To act in a way that draws attention to you and makes you seem attractive.

gay Sexually or romantically attracted to people of the same sex.

individuality Traits that make a person unique and special.

peer pressure When people your age, often friends or classmates, pressure you to do something that you wouldn't normally do.

rejection The state of being cast off.

sexually transmitted diseases (STDs) Diseases transmitted through sexual contact, including AIDS, genital herpes, syphilis, and gonorrhea.

American Social Health Association
P.O. Box 13827
Research Triangle Park, NC 27709
(919) 361-8400
Web site: http//www.ashastd.org
   The American Social Health Association Web site contains
   information about STDs, including descriptions of diseases, their symptoms, and manner of transmission. There
   is also information about prevention and instruction
   regarding birth control and safe sex practices.

Domestic Violence Hotline
(800) 799-SAFE (7233)

Go Ask Alice
Web site: http//www.goaskalice.columbia.edu
   The Go Ask Alice Web site offers advice and information
   about a range of topics related to sexuality in straight-
   forward language. This site encourages discussion and
   education in a setting where kids interact with their peers.

Planned Parenthood Federation of America
434 West 33rd Street
New York, NY 10001
(800) 230-PLAN (7526)
(212) 541-7800
Web site: http//www.plannedparenthood.org

The Planned Parenthood Web site provides a directory of the Planned Parenthood health centers, information about reproductive health for men and women, and a link to teenwire.com, a reproductive health Web site friendly to kids and Spanish speakers.

Rape, Abuse, and Incest National Network (RAINN)
2000 L Street NW, Suite 406
Washington, DC 20036
(800) 656-HOPE (4673)
Web site: http//www.rainn.org
e-mail: RAINNmail@aol.com
  RAINN's Web site offers educational programs designed to prevent sexual abuse, statistics about abuse, directions to counseling centers, and a toll-free counseling phone line.

Sexuality Information and Education Council of the United States (SIECUS)
130 West 42nd Street, Suite 350
New York, NY 10036
(212) 819-9770
Web site: http//www.siecus.org
  The SEICUS Web site offers information on sexuality, including health, worldwide policy and educational programs, and links to other sexuality-related Web sites.

Web Sites

Due to the changing nature of Internet links, Rosen Publishing has developed an online list of Web sites related to the subject of this book. This site is updated regularly. Please use this link to access the list:

http://www.rosenlinks.com/faq/dati

For Further Reading

Anderson, Laurie Halse. *Speak.* New York, NY: Penguin
Putnam Books for Young Readers, 1999.

Bell, Ruth. *Changing Bodies, Changing Lives: A Book for
Teens on Sex and Relationships.* New York, NY: Times
Books, 1998.

Cohn, Rachel, and David Levithan. *Nick and Norah's
Infinite Playlist.* New York, NY: Knopf, 2006.

Dessen, Sarah. *The Truth About Forever.* New York, NY:
Viking, 2006.

Levy, Barrie. *In Love and in Danger: A Teen's Guide to
Breaking Free of Abusive Relationships.* Seattle, WA:
Seal Press, 1998.

Pinsky, Drew, et al. *The Dr. Drew and Adam Book: A Survival
Guide to Life and Love.* New York, NY: Dell, 1998.

Bibliography

About.com. "Teen Advice: Before You Make that Date."
Retrieved May 2, 2006 (http://teenadvice.about.com/cs/
lovedating/bb/blbigdate.htm).

Cloud, Henry, and John Townsend. *Boundaries in Dating
Particant's Guide*. Grand Rapids, MI: Zondervan
Publishing House, 2001.

Hatchell, Deborah. *What Smart Teenagers Know About
Dating, Relationships, and Sex*. Santa Barbara, CA: Piper
Books, 2003.

Hovanec, Erin M. *The Need to Know Library: Everything
You Need to Know About Dating and Relationships*. New
York, NY: The Rosen Publishing Group, Inc., 2000.

Kolyer, Diane. *The Need to Know Library: Everything You
Need to Know About Dating*. New York, NY: The Rosen
Publishing Group, 2005

Packer, Alex J. *The How Rude! Handbook of Friendship &
Dating Manners for Teens: Surviving the Social Scene*.
Minneapolis, MN: Free Spirit Publishing, Inc., 2004.

National Youth Violence Prevention Resource Center. "Teen
Dating Violence." Retrieved May 2, 2006 (http://www.
safeyouth.org/scripts/teens/dating.asp).

Index

Photo Credits

Series Designer: Evelyn Horovicz